FRANK CLUNE'S
NED KELLY

Illustrated by WALTER STACKPOOL

ANGUS & ROBERTSON PUBLISHERS

IN *1840 there lived in Ireland a young gamekeeper named John Kelly. He was employed by Lord Ormonde, a wealthy aristocrat who owned the estate of Killarney. A farmer who lived in the Golden Vale of Tipperary complained to the police that two pigs, valued at ten shillings each, had been stolen from his farm. The police were soon on the trail and arrested John Kelly on suspicion of theft. On 1st January 1841 John, aged twenty-one, was found guilty by a jury and sentenced to seven years' transportation to Australia.*

After several months in gaol, John Kelly was placed on board the convict ship Prince Regent *with 182 fellow-convicts, shackled and manacled hand and foot. They were bound for Van Diemen's Land, later known as Tasmania, and few, if any, ever returned to the land of their birth. Almost one year after John Kelly's conviction the* Prince Regent *dropped anchor in the Derwent River, hard by the port of Hobart.*

John Kelly served his sentence for seven years on the island. When at last he was set free he raised the fare to pay his passage to the mainland of Australia, and farewelled Van Diemen's Land for ever.

After crossing Bass Strait in a sailing ship, John Kelly, known as Red, arrived in Melbourne the capital of the Port Phillip district. He found work as a bush carpenter and met Ellen Quinn, an attractive lass aged eighteen, daughter of struggling Irish migrants from County Antrim. It was love at first sight between Red and Ellen, but her parents did not approve of a son-in-law who had been a convict and had served his time in Van Diemen's Land.

But the lovers eloped on horseback to Melbourne, one jump ahead of Ellen's furious parents. In June 1855 a male child was born to Ellen. This tiny infant was "Edward", soon to be "Ned".

Young Ned Kelly

Ned began life in times of turmoil, defiance of the law, and rebellion. His boyhood would be wild, wide and free — not for him the advantages of a gentleman's education and opportunities. Ned would have to take life in the raw. But he was a happy baby, stumbling after his father, who was now a quiet, decent citizen working hard as a fencer and carpenter.

John Kelly moved his family to Avenel, a small village eighty miles north of Melbourne on the busy Sydney Road in order to get away from his wife's troublesome relatives. Here he started a dairy. Ned was old enough now to go to school, and here he learnt his three Rs — reading, 'riting, and 'rithmetic — from the schoolmaster, Richardson. He was a bright pupil, and well-behaved.

But his father was to meet misfortune. On 28th May 1865 John Kelly made a desperate effort to get food for his hungry family, now six children. He killed a heifer-calf that had strayed into his paddock. Next day his neighbour, Morgan, told the police. A search-warrant was issued against John Kelly. Constable Doxey found part of a heifer hanging on a hook and, worse still, the hide of the beast was found under the bed with Morgan's brand cut out. On 29th May 1865, at Avenel police-station, John Kelly was fined £25 or six months in prison with hard labour.

At the time of this heavy blow John Kelly was forty-five and had ''gone straight'' ever since he was released from his convict sentence. Only twice in his life had he stolen, each time for food. A kindly neighbour paid the fine, and he was released from gaol. Two months later, on 10th August 1865, Ellen gave birth to her seventh child. On 27th December John Kelly, who had been ill for some time, died from consumption. Ned, the eldest son, who was now nearly twelve, had to go to the police-station to sign the form for his father's death, and now took on all the worries and responsibilities of the family.

While still only twelve years old Ned achieved local fame for a deed of courage. A farmer, who was a neighbour of the Kellys, fell into a creek and was on the verge of drowning when young Ned plunged into the river, swam out to the man and pulled him to the bank. The brave rescue became the talk of the countryside.

Some time after the death of his father his mother made a decision that was to alter Ned's whole life. She decided to leave

Avenel and move back to her family, the Quinns. Her father, now living at Glenmore, thirty miles south-east of Benalla, arranged for a home for his daughter and her children not far away at Eleven Mile Creek. Ned left school and, without a father or schoolmaster to guide him, fell into bad company. He was influenced by the talk and behaviour of Uncle Jimmy Quinn (who had been in prison and was known as "The Wild One") and his mates, bragging about how they would "get even" with the police. Everyone seemed determined to get square with the policemen who had put them behind bars, for they all felt unjustly imprisoned. Ned, a high-spirited, intelligent boy, began to see things their way.

A Scrape with the Law

Real trouble struck the Kelly family on 14th October 1869, when Ned was fourteen. A Chinese hawker named Ah Fook stopped at Mrs

Kelly's house and asked for a drink of water. He could easily have got it from the creek, but it was said that he was a police informer and was trying to find out whether Ellen Kelly sold liquor. Since she had no licence to do so, this would have been against the law. Ned's sister Anne offered Ah Fook a pannikin of water from the creek, the hawker tasted it, spat it out, and began waving his arms wildly.

Anne told him to go away, but Ah Fook went on waving his arms furiously and shouting loudly at her. Ned, working close by in the paddock, came over to his sister, and asked why Ah Fook was so excited.

"He's insulting me!" said Anne.

"Clear out!" said Ned to Ah Fook.

Ah Fook angrily turned on Ned, waving a bamboo stick. The boy took it from him, belted him on the shins, and chased him away down the road.

Ah Fook went screeching down the road, reached Benalla, and reported the assault to the police. The following day Sergeant Whelan arrived at Eleven Mile Creek, arrested Ned Kelly, and took him to the Benalla lock-up.

Next morning, 16th October 1869, Ned was placed in the dock before a Justice of the Peace, charged with robbery and violence. Sergeant Whelan stated that the prisoner had robbed Ah Fook of ten shillings and threatened to beat him to death.

Young Kelly was remanded, without bail, and locked up. Five days later he was brought before the Justice of the Peace again. A further remand was granted. Ned was returned to prison for a further ten days. On 26th October a magistrate dismissed the charge.

"There is nothing to go before a jury," he said. "I discharge the prisoner."

The prosecution had failed — but from now on, in the eyes of the police, Ned was a "juvenile bushranger".

Highway Robbery

About this time Harry Power, an escaped convict, was engaged in the profession of robbery under arms. Convicted in 1855 for stealing horses, he had nearly served his sentence of fourteen years when, a couple of months before his release, he escaped and became a bushranger — a "polite" bushranger, who respected women, and joked with his victims, after he had taken their wallets and watches. A superb horseman, Power easily threw off police pursuit, though the police were eager to collect the £500 offered for his capture. Power's hide-out was in dense scrub in the Kelly country, where he seemed to be able to get plenty of food, and also the tip-off when mounted troopers were around. For about a year after his escape he was a lone prowler; then, early in 1870, it was noticed that he had a mate, a mounted youth who stayed a little distance from the scene of Power's stick-ups, and held his horse ready for a quick get-away.

The young accomplice was Ned Kelly.

Power's secret camp was on a hill about a mile from the homestead, and he had made a pact with the Quinns for their help and provisions. It was Uncle Jimmy Quinn who had persuaded Ned, who was trying desperately to earn enough money to keep his mother, brothers and sisters, that he should join Power as his offsider.

On 5th May 1870 Ned Kelly, aged fifteen, was arrested for "highway robbery under arms". On 12th May people gathered at the Benalla Court House "to find out the fate of Edward Kelly, charged with two separate counts of highway robbery".

The magistrate dismissed the case for lack of evidence. The police, however, had the boy remanded, stating "Ned Kelly had been concerned in a highway robbery under arms with Power".

And so the supposed juvenile bushranger was manacled to the police coach, taken to Kyneton under heavy armed guard, and held in custody. He remained in prison until 23rd June, when the case against him was again dismissed for lack of evidence. But he had been held a prisoner for seven weeks, which was the idea of a clever police officer who thought that he could get information about Power from Ned. Surely he would be willing to sell the bushranger for £500? But Ned was not willing and said nothing.

Several months passed, until October 1870, when Ned was charged with assaulting a neighbour and sentenced to three months' gaol. In the same Court he was given a further three months, on a second charge arising from the same incident.

When he was released and arrived home he had an unlucky home-coming. Wild Wright, a neighbour, had borrowed a chestnut horse at Mansfield and rode to Mrs Kelly's for a spree, then left, asking the Kellys to mind the horse until his return. Ned innocently rode the borrowed horse into Greta, where he was pounced upon by Constable Hall, torn off his horse, knocked unconscious by five men, handcuffed by Hall, trussed hand and foot, and taken to Wangaratta. Tried on a charge of receiving a stolen horse, he was found guilty, and sentenced to three years' hard labour at Pentridge gaol. Ned was then sixteen.

In February 1874 Ned Kelly was released from prison. He was a few months under nineteen years of age. When he had entered the gaol he was a beardless lad; but no razor caressed his chin at Pentridge and he had a well-grown beard. Apart from the beard, his face showed the effects of the heavy punishment he had endured — unjustly, he still believed. There was a sullen look, a desperation in his eyes — a great change from the keen and sensitive face he had before.

Ned Kelly was a desperado, with a chip on his shoulder. From the moment he was released, he was at war with the community that had spoilt his life.

There was now a railway-line linking Melbourne with Glenrowan, a few miles from Greta. Ned alighted from the train at Glenrowan and hurried along the bush track to his house, and the fond, tearful welcome waiting for him there.

After working for almost two years in a sawmill, which eventually had to close down, Ned went prospecting for gold on the King River. But he had no luck.

Horse Stealing

Out of work, he began horse and cattle duffing — stealing horses and cattle from squatters and driving them across the Murray River into New South Wales, where there was a ready market for stolen goods.

Several months passed, in which Ned had some minor trouble with the police, and his brother, Dan, aged fifteen, was found "not guilty of stealing a saddle and bridle". The police awaited their chance and issued another warrant for Dan's arrest, this time for cattle and horse duffing.

The 15th of April 1878 was a day of disaster for the Kelly family and the police of Victoria. On that day Constable Fitzpatrick rode from Benalla to Greta, a journey of fifteen miles.

Arriving at Greta, he asked Ellen Kelly, "Is Dan at home?"

At that moment Dan entered.

"What do you want?" he asked.

"There's a charge against you for stealing horses at Chiltern."

According to Constable Fitzpatrick, when he made this statement he was attacked by Ned and Dan Kelly and all their relatives, who attempted to murder him. Somehow he managed to escape and reached Benalla where he told his story.

Next day, Sergeant Steele and two policemen arrived at Greta, and arrested Ellen Kelly and two of her friends. On 9th October, at Beechworth, nearly five months later, they were charged with aiding and abetting an attempt to murder Constable Fitzpatrick. On the sole evidence of Fitzpatrick, the jury found them guilty.

Said the judge, Sir Redmond Barry, to Mrs Kelly, "If your son Ned were here, I would make an example of him. I would give him a sentence of fifteen years."

After gaoling Ellen Kelly, the police thought of a plan to capture Ned and his comrades in crime. Four police, disguised as gold prospectors, rode from Mansfield to the Wombat Ranges and made camp at Stringybark Creek, seventeen miles away. This was to be their base camp while they made armed patrols in search of the wanted men.

Murder

On 25th October Sergeant Kennedy and Constables Lonigan, Scanlon and McIntyre rode to Stringybark Creek and made camp.

But Ned had already seen them. He wrote later: "I crossed their tracks and rode to our camp, and told my brother and his mates." His brother was Dan, and his mates Joe Byrne, aged twenty-one, and Steve Hart, aged eighteen. At twenty-three, Ned was the natural leader because of his superior strength, his intelligence and his reckless courage.

On Saturday, 26th October, Sergeant Kennedy and Constable Scanlon mounted their horses and went on patrol, leaving Lonigan and McIntyre to hold the fort. While Lonigan was in the tent making bread McIntyre shot parrots, a sure sign that the police had no idea the Kellys were nearby. A grave error . . .

Creeping up to the camp, Ned shouted, "Bail up! Put up your hands!" McIntyre obeyed, but Lonigan, a brave man, drew his revolver — and one of the Kelly Gang shot him dead. McIntyre surrendered. Then into the picture rode Kennedy and Scanlon. McIntyre shouted a warning.

"You had better surrender, sergeant, we are surrounded!"

Kennedy, thinking it was a joke, put his hand on his revolver as Kelly shouted, "Put up your hands!"

Kennedy leapt off his horse and took cover behind a fallen tree, and Scanlon spurred forward, unslinging his rifle. As he did so Kelly fired his shot-gun and Scanlon fell dead. McIntyre, in terror, leapt on Scanlon's horse and bolted away through the bush to Mansfield to report the murders. Ned and Dan started a grim duel with Kennedy, a brave man who refused to surrender, but dodged from tree to tree, firing his revolver, reloading, and firing again. One of Kennedy's bullets grazed Dan's shoulder, another went through Ned's beard. The fight continued until Kennedy fell, struck below the armpit by a bullet fired by Ned. He was seriously wounded and could not move. As night came on Ned saw that he would probably not survive his injuries and, on an impulse, which he may have thought kind and humane, decided that he could not leave him at the mercy of the dingoes. He shot Kennedy through the heart.

Then he walked back to the camp, got Kennedy's overcoat, and covered him with it as a sign of respect for a brave foe.

When the news of the murders reached Melbourne the Government proclaimed the Kelly Gang as outlaws, and offered a reward of £500 for each of them, dead or alive. Over two hundred policemen were drafted into the district, and scores of Kelly friends were arrested and held in gaol for weeks while the police tried to find out the outlaws' hiding-place.

Bank Robbery

Ned now decided to be an outlaw in earnest. To maintain supplies of arms and food he needed money, so he decided to rob a bank.

He chose the bank at Euroa and decided that the right moment for a robbery would be when the court was in session. He reasoned that few people would be in the streets on a mid-summer afternoon, when most would either be at home or in the Court House. He had also found that there was only one foot-constable stationed at Euroa to protect the bank, post office, railway station, two or three hotels, and all the stores. Despite several warnings, the police had made no attempt to get more of their men stationed in Euroa, though they knew the Kellys were at large.

Having completed their preparations, the four outlaws, mounted on splendid horses, rode towards Euroa with every detail of the robbery worked out in advance. They dismounted at Faithfull's Creek sheep-station, four miles from Euroa. Ned and his mates went to the kitchen door and spoke to Fitzgerald, a rouseabout, and his wife, the housekeeper. His first words rocked them.

"I'm Ned Kelly," he said. He had a revolver in his hand, but he did not point it at them. "You'll have to bail up, but we won't hurt you if you do as you're told. We'd like to have some dinner."

"Of course, Mr Kelly, come in!" said the housekeeper.

The outlaws sat at the table enjoying a hearty meal. Mrs Fitzgerald was impressed by their polite manners, and Ned won her motherly sympathy at once by telling her how badly his own mother and sisters had been treated by the police.

Later Ned and Byrne walked to the stables with Fitzgerald while Dan and Hart fetched the horses.

"Do you know who I am?" Ned asked the groom.

"Ned Kelly!" said the groom, trying to be funny.

"You're a good guesser," said Ned, producing his revolver. "Bail up!"

The groom paled, and held up his hands.

"I beg your pardon," he gasped. "I was only joking."

"I can take a joke," said Ned. "But we want some feed for our horses."

"Certainly," said the groom. "There's plenty of oats and chaff here."

For the rest of the day and night Ned and his gang held everyone prisoner, capturing, but not hurting, the various men as they returned to the homestead. A lantern was lit and kept burning all night, and the sixteen prisoners lay on the floor, smoking or dozing. For several hours Ned sat inside, too, talking in a friendly way and answering the many questions they asked him about his encounters with the police. He was an entertaining story-teller and kept his audience enthralled. He even told them that the gang intended to rob the bank the next day, and that the purpose in sticking up Faithfull's Creek was to give their horses a good feed overnight, so that they would be fresh for a quick get-away after the bank had been robbed.

Next day the outlaws took their horses out of the stables and turned them out to graze in the house paddock. Then they harnessed a covered wagon and a spring-cart, helped themselves to a brand-new outfit of clothes from a hawker they were holding prisoner, collected some ammunition, and set out for Euroa. They arrived at four o'clock. The street was deserted, the town drowsy in the heat. Ned and Hart entered the bank while Dan went round to the back door.

"I'm Ned Kelly!" said Ned. "I am an outlaw, and my orders must be obeyed. Make no noise. Raise no alarm. Keep your hands up and stand against the wall."

Hart was soon joined by Dan, and they kept everyone covered at gun-point while Ned filled a sugar-bag with gold and silver coins, banknotes and about 31 ounces of unminted gold. The total haul was about £2000, and the raid had taken only half an hour.

Their prisoners were then taken out to the covered wagon — including the bank manager's wife and children, in case they gave the alarm — and driven back to Faithfull's Creek. Here they were held captive with the other members of the homestead. Supper was served to the outlaws and their captives in the cool of the evening, then the brigands saddled their horses and prepared to depart. Before doing so they entertained their guests to an astonishing display of trick-riding in

the house paddock, picking up handkerchiefs from the ground at full gallop, jumping stiff fences, and generally showing off.

At about half past eight, as the last flicker of twilight faded, the outlaws rode away, with the money and gold from the Euroa bank safely strapped to their horses.

News of the bank robbery created intense excitement, and on 13th December 1878 the Government increased the reward to £1000 on each of the outlaws. Now for the first time Stephen Hart and Joseph Byrne were named as part of the Kelly Gang.

After hiding for a few weeks in one of their camps, the four popped up again in Jerilderie, thirty miles north of the Murray River in New South Wales.

At about 10 p.m., when all lights except the jewelled glitter of the stars had faded from the sky, the bandits rode quietly into the township. A couple of hundred yards from the police-station three of them tethered their horses and advanced on foot. Ned spurred his horse to a gallop along the road. There was no light showing at the police-station. The occupants were all in bed.

Dismounting, Ned knocked at the front door and called out in a tone of great excitement, "Mr Devine! Come quickly! There's been a murder at Davidson's Hotel, at Billabong Creek."

Awakened, Constable Devine lit a lantern, and opened the door.

"I'm Ned Kelly!" said Ned, suddenly showing a revolver in each hand. "Bail up! Put up your hands! Stand still or I'll shoot."

From the darkness the other three bandits rushed forward with revolvers. All went inside and the front door was closed. Ned assured the policemen and their families that they would not be hurt.

Dan then found some handcuffs and gleefully manacled the police, who were put in the lock-up for the night. Next morning the outlaws dressed themselves in police uniform — and not one of the people living in Jerilderie had the slightest idea what had happened.

During the next few hours they took everyone prisoner in the Royal Hotel nearby and put them all in the dining-room under armed guard. Then they robbed the bank. And when they returned to the Royal Hotel, Ned, a bearded young outlaw in police uniform, told his captive audience the terrible story of his life in words of fierce sincerity and power, mixed with sarcasm and humour. Then the Kelly Gang galloped away singing, "Hurrah for the good old days of Morgan and Ben Hall!"

Suits of Armour

For some reason best known to themselves they stopped their war against the law for more than sixteen months. But the law continued in its efforts to capture the Kellys. The Government in Melbourne had

asked the Queensland Government for a party of black trackers to help in the hunt for the Kelly Gang. The nervous strain of dodging these invisible pursuers affected Ned's morale and judgment.

Early in 1880 the police were told that mould-boards of ploughs had been stolen from the neighbourhood of Greta and Oxley. They did not know, and could not guess, what was the purpose of these strange thefts, but they sent search parties with black trackers, to investigate. The trackers discovered marks of high-heeled riding-boots — known as "larrikin heels" — near the farms where the mould-boards had been stolen. From this the police felt sure that the Kelly Gang were the thieves, since they were known to wear larrikin-heeled boots.

At a hide-out in the Greta Swamps, Ned and his mates heated the metal mould-boards and hammered them over a green log to a round shape, to protect their bodies in the pitched battle with the police which they believed must come soon. Each suit of armour consisted of two main sections, front and back; these were held together at the sides by leather laces, and supported from the shoulders by strong straps. An apron made from part of a mould-board was attached to the edge of the front-piece by bolt and swivel to protect the groin and thighs. The weight of the armour suits was about eighty pounds, a heavy load for these slightly built youths to carry. Only one helmet was made — for Ned, who had the physical strength to carry the extra weight of fifteen pounds.

After the successful raid on Jerilderie, the Government of New South Wales offered a reward of £1000 each for the bodies of the outlaws, dead or alive. This, added to the Victorian offer, meant a grand total of £8000. But where were they? Months passed, a year passed, while informers, greedy for the reward, passed information to the police. One informer was Aaron Sherritt, who was engaged to Byrne's sister. His informing cost him his life. He was spotted entering a police camp. On Saturday, 27th June 1880, though guarded in his home by four constables, Sherritt was shot dead by Byrne and Dan Kelly.

Ned Kelly was realising that his days were also numbered. For £8000 friends could become enemies. He began to make plans.

Attack on the Police Train

He guessed that when news of the death of Sherritt reached

Melbourne, a train carrying police officers would be sent to Glenrowan. He was right.

At about one o'clock in the morning, by moonlight, Ned and Steve Hart arrived at the spot where they intended to wreck the train — three-quarters of a mile from Glenrowan railway station, where there was a curve in the line, with an embankment thirty to forty feet high.

Leaving their horses and armour in a clump of trees, Ned and Steve tried with hand-spanners to take up some of the rails, but the nuts were rusted and could not be budged. At any moment the two desperados expected the special train to arrive. It was a cold and frosty morning in midwinter, and Ned and Hart, wearing overcoats, ran along the line to Glenrowan station, hoping to find there the proper tools for lifting the rails.

Near the level crossing, a gang of eight navvies were camped in tents. Ned and Hart bailed them up, and then knocked on the gatehouse door. The station-master, Stanistreet, came to the door. Ned ordered him to get dressed and direct the men to remove the rails. They protested that it was a platelayer's job. Cursing at the loss of time, Ned left the prisoners with Hart and went off to find the platelayers.

After many delays, which included getting the platelayers' wives and children out of bed and dressed — for no one could be left behind to raise the alarm — they walked in the frosty moonlight back to the gatehouse, guarded by the worried Ned.

Hart, in the meantime, had forced the station-master to find the right tools, and now angry words passed between Ned and the platelayers when they were told to tear up the rails. The crime they were being asked to carry out made their blood run cold. They delayed as long as they dared, but they knew very well that Ned Kelly was not a man to be trifled with.

Presently Joe Byrne and Dan arrived, after their long night ride from Sherritt's home.

But the train did not arrive . . .

As the people of the township were beginning to wake up, a new plan had to be quickly made. It was important to prevent any warning being sent to Benalla or Wangaratta. No one could be allowed to leave Glenrowan.

As the sun came up, the prisoners were taken to Mrs Jones's hotel. The lady, obeying Ned's orders, opened the bar and made the prisoners welcome — and anyone in the township who stirred out of doors was grabbed and added to the group. The postmaster was grabbed early to prevent him from sending telegrams, but Constable Bracken, at the police-station, was sick in bed and had no idea that anything unusual was happening.

The hours passed. During the morning the armour was brought in and placed in a room which the outlaws kept for themselves.

The train still did not arrive.

Foolishly, the outlaws began to drink in the bar with the prisoners, and when darkness fell Ned allowed some of the residents to go home. Among those he trusted — for he had told everyone of his plan to wreck the train — was the schoolmaster, Curnow, and his family.

"Go home and don't dream too loud," Ned told him.

Then as a further safety precaution Ned and Byrne went to the police-station and "arrested" Constable Bracken, bringing him to the hotel.

Towards dawn, Ned decided that his plans to wreck the train had failed.

"Everyone can go home now," he announced.

But at that very moment there was a long shrieking whistle in the distance. The train, laden with police, had left Benalla, and was thundering towards Glenrowan — at last!

Hurriedly the four outlaws buckled on their armour.

But when the train was about one and a half miles from the station the driver saw a red light flickering dimly ahead on the moonlit track. He blew a long blast on his whistle.

The train came to a standstill. What was wrong?

There, standing between the rails, was the schoolmaster, Tom Curnow, holding a lighted candle behind a red scarf. This moment he knew would be the most dangerous in his life, for the white light of the candle on his face would make him an easy mark for the Kelly Gang.

But his luck held — and he gasped out his story.

The battle of Glenrowan was about to begin.

Battle of Glenrowan

Back at the hotel, Ned, dressed in his armour, addressed the prisoners.

"Anybody who leaves the hotel will be shot," he said grimly.

But when no one was looking, Constable Bracken unlocked the front door and ran towards the railway station. His courage was superb. Four expert marksmen, armed with rifles, were behind him. But they did not see him. When Bracken reached the railway platform he called out: "The Kellys! The Kellys! Here in Glenrowan. In Mrs Jones's hotel. Hurry!"

Had Superintendent Hare paused a moment to form up his men and give them orders to throw a cordon round the hotel, things might have been different, but he thought only of storming the hotel by a frontal charge.

"Come on men, follow me! Let the horses go!"

At this moment, the outlaws, encased in their armour beneath their overcoats, came round the end of the hotel. Their plan had been to sneak forward and attack the police at the railway station. Instead, they saw the sixteen policemen advancing towards them.

Hare halted at thirty paces and, seeing the figures in the shadows, called out, "Don't be foolish. I want to speak to you!"

Ned's voice boomed back in reply: "I don't want to speak to you!"

Hare discharged both barrels of his shot-gun. The other police opened fire at the figures in armour. The four outlaws, all armed with rifles, returned the fire in a hot volley.

With his first shot Ned Kelly sent a rifle bullet through Hare's wrist, but a bullet also struck Ned in the left forearm. This was the most decisive shot in the whole battle, for it prevented Ned from using his Spencer repeating rifle, which must be supported by the left arm. He was also struck in the upper part of the arm, and also his foot. Most fatal of all, the heavy armour destroyed the outlaws' freedom of movement.

Ned, bleeding freely, hopped round to the north side of the hotel. The other three went through the front door into the hotel. It was not Ned's idea that his gang should take shelter behind the people imprisoned there.

"Come out!" he yelled to Byrne. But they did not appear.

Then Ned decided on a bold stroke to draw the police away from the hotel. He staggered into the stockyard and tried to mount a horse, but it was impossible in his armour, so he lurched away into the bush where his grey mare was tethered. There he sat down and tried to unfasten his armour, but because of his injured hands he could not get the bolts undone. After much struggling, he eased the helmet off his head. Next he tried to load the rifle, but could not do that, either. He decided to lie hidden in the bush for a while, so he untethered his mare and let her go. This was a bad decision, for Ned now had no way of retreat.

Feeling very weak, he put on his helmet again, but forgot to put on the padded skull-cap his sisters had made for him. He lay, half fainting from loss of blood. Footsteps were coming towards him! Would he be found? But the policemen were thinking only of surrounding the hotel, and did not look in the bushes where Ned lay hidden.

Kelly's Courage

After lying encased in his armour on the frosty ground for three and a half hours, Ned came fully to his senses and decided to return to battle. Desperately wounded as he was, weakened by loss of blood, his limbs frozen and encumbered by nearly a hundredweight of iron, he managed to stand up and walk — not away from the fight, in the direction of safety for himself, but back to the hotel to rescue his mates.

It was at that moment and by that decision, that Ned Kelly's name was fixed in Australia's lore as a symbol of reckless courage.

As game as Ned Kelly . . .

This was the supreme moment of his life, and perhaps he knew it.

It was one of the policemen who first noticed the seemingly gigantic figure lurching among the saplings. In the mist and smoke-fog, just before sun-up, the approaching figure, clad in a long grey overcoat over the armour, and wearing the rounded helmet with a slit in it, appeared to be about nine feet tall.

"It's the Bunyip! It's Old Nick!" yelled somebody.

The police opened fire, aiming at its head and chest. The bullets struck with a metallic clang. The tall figure staggered at each impact but continued to advance. A loud muffled voice came from the slit in the helmet.

"Fire away, you can't hurt me!"

The police closed in rapidly, firing at the outlaw's legs and arms, and a charge of gunshot fired by Sergeant Steele finally brought him crashing to the ground. The police seized his wrist and wrenched the revolver from him. Then they pulled off his helmet.

"My God, it's Ned!"

Sergeant Steele grabbed the outlaw by the beard and drew his revolver.

"You wretch!" he shouted. "I swore I'd be in at your death, and I am!"

"Take him alive!" yelled another man.

Constable Bracken pushed Steele's revolver aside.

"If you shoot him, I'll shoot you," he said.

They were not more than sixty yards from the hotel where Dan and Hart could have fired upon them with deadly effect if they had chosen. But those two dazed and drink-stupefied youths did not take this opportunity of helping Ned. And so the outlaw was carried to the railway station and placed on a mattress in the station-master's office. There the police tried to persuade Ned to make his mates surrender — but he knew they never would, and there was nothing he could do.

At about 10 a.m., after the police had been firing at the hotel for about seven hours, the order was given to cease fire. A strange silence settled on the scene. No shots came from the hotel.

Then a loud voice called from the police positions: "We will give you ten minutes. All innocent persons to come out."

After about three minutes the people who had been kept prisoner at the hotel came out.

"Keep your hands up! Come this way! Keep your hands up!"

Everyone was identified, searched and questioned, and the police learnt for the first time that Joe Byrne was dead. The other two, still wearing their armour, were apparently quiet and miserable and talking together in low tones. They knew that Ned was captured and that their own position was hopeless.

The police now decided to set fire to the hotel and smoke them out. Under a heavy burst of fire, a policeman ran forward with a bundle of straw and placed it against the weatherboard wall. He struck a match and lit the straw. The rifle-fire ceased. As the flames licked at the wall, fanned by the southerly breeze, a hush of awe fell on the spectators. Now or never the outlaws must emerge.

Dean Gibney, a Roman Catholic priest, who happened to be on the train, and who had already spoken with Ned, now showed great personal heroism.

"May God protect me," he said. "I'm going into that house, to give those men a chance to have a little time to prepare themselves before they die."

And as the flames crackled and black smoke billowed, he walked forward alone into the burning building.

"In the name of God," he called to the outlaws, "I am a Catholic priest. Do not shoot me."

Inside he ran quickly from room to room. He saw the dead body of Joe Byrne, and then in a little room at the back he saw two bodies lying side by side on the floor. Their armour was off and laid beside them. They were Dan Kelly and Steve Hart. They had been dead for some time and it appeared they had committed suicide. The priest emerged and told the police what he had found. A few minutes later the hotel became a raging mass of flames.

So the Kelly Gang was ended in that strange battle which lasted for twelve and a half hours on Monday, 28th June 1880.

Ned's Trial

Ned Kelly was taken by the police to Melbourne Gaol hospital, and carefully nursed back to health. On 28th October 1880 he was put on trial. A jury was chosen, evidence was heard, and the "twelve good men and true" gave their verdict — guilty.

The judge, Sir Redmond Barry, asked the formal question, "Prisoner at the bar, have you anything to say why sentence of death should not be passed upon you?"

Ned looked at the judge thoughtfully.

"Well," he said, "it is rather too late for me to speak now. I wish I had insisted on examining the witnesses myself. I could have thrown a different light on the case — but I thought if I did so it would look like bravado and flashiness."

This interruption of the death sentence was something quite new. Ned continued to argue quietly and coolly with the judge. At last he said, "A day will come, at a bigger Court than this, when we shall see which is right and which is wrong. No matter how long a man lives, he has to come to judgment somewhere. If I had examined the witnesses, I would have stopped a lot of the reward, I assure you!"

After a few more exchanges, the judge decided to bring the fantastic argument to a close. He looked at his notes, prepared in advance, and read in solemn tones a homily on the miseries of an outlaw's lot and on Ned's misdeeds. He ended by pronouncing the sentence: "You will be taken from here to the place from whence you came, and thence to a place of execution, and there you will be hanged by the neck until you be dead, and may the Lord have mercy on your soul!"

Ned looked fixedly at the ageing judge.

"I will add something to that," he said, as the Court listened in awe-struck silence. "I will see you where I am going!"

Many people remembered these words when Sir Redmond Barry was suddenly taken ill two days after Ned was hanged, and died soon afterwards.

The date fixed for Ned's execution was 11th November 1880. On the day before his brothers and sisters were allowed to visit him, and after this, his mother. Her last words to him were: "Mind you die like a Kelly, Ned!"

The morning of Thursday, 11th November, dawned fine and clear. Ned was taken to the gallows. As the hangman adjusted the noose Ned looked round him resignedly and said, "Ah well, I suppose it has to come to this!"

A white cap was put over his head and face. As it was pulled down over his eyes Ned spoke three words, with a sigh:

"Such is life!"